THE GREATEST ADVENTURES IN THE WORLD

David
AND GOLIATH

TONY BRADMAN & TONY ROSS

ORCHARD

ORCHARD BOOKS

The text was first published in Great Britain in a gift collection called
The Orchard Book of Heroes and Villains with full colour illustrations by Tony Ross, in 2008
This edition first published in hardback in 2010
First paperback publication in 2011

3 5 7 9 10 8 6 4 2
Text © Tony Bradman 2008
Illustrations © Tony Ross 2010

A CIP catalogue record for this book is available from the British Library.

ISBN 978 1 40830 578 2

Printed and bound in Germany by GGP Media GmbH, Poessneck

The paper and board used in this book are made from wood from responsible sources

Orchard Books
An imprint of Hachette Children's Group
Part of The Watts Publishing Group Limited
Carmelite House, 50 Victoria Embankment, London EC4Y 0DZ

An Hachette UK Company
www.hachette.co.uk
www.hachettechildrens.co.uk

CONTENTS

CHAPTER ONE

DAVID

ONCE, LONG AGO IN THE ancient, troubled land of Judea, there was a boy called David. He was the youngest son of Jesse, a farmer who lived in Bethlehem, a small village in the hills.

Jesse had eight sons all told, and being the youngest had its problems. David loved his brothers, but to them he was the baby of the family, and they often made fun of him.

At that time, David's people – the Israelites – were at war with the Philistines, a tribe of fierce fighters. One day, news came to Jesse's farm that the Philistines had marched deep into the heart of the Israelites' land. The future of Judea was at stake, and David's brothers stepped forward to volunteer for battle.

"Hey, count me in too!" said David when he heard what was happening. His job was to look after the family's sheep, and he had just brought the flock in from the hills for the night. "I definitely want to go."

"Don't be stupid," said his oldest brother, Eliab. "It will be men's work, David – proper fighting, not some pretend adventure for a little boy."

"I'm not a little boy," said David. "I'm nearly grown-up, and I'm tired of you lot treating me like a child. You'll let me go, Father, won't you?"

Jesse had always had a soft spot for his youngest son, and sometimes indulged his wishes. But on this occasion Jesse agreed with his firstborn.

"No, I'm sorry, David," he said. "Eliab is right – you're just not old enough to be a warrior. Your day will come…"

For a second, David felt like arguing, and running off to sulk. But instead he helped his brothers gather their weapons and armour, and load their packhorses with food and drink.

They left the next
morning, and David
took the family's
flock back to the
hills. Then he sat
under a tree and brooded
as the animals bleated and nibbled at the
juicy grass.

How could he
become a man if
things carried
on this way?
His father
and brothers
never gave
him a
chance.

He hated the thought that while his brothers were going to fight for their people, he would be stuck at home doing nothing more than looking after a bunch of smelly woolly-backs. Although being a shepherd wasn't exactly a child's game.

There were often threats to the flock. Why, this winter alone David had fought off jackals, a couple of wolves, and a hungry lion that had come sniffing down the cold wind for prey. He had even had to kill a huge bear.

The creature had attacked at twilight on a misty evening. David had whipped out his trusty sling, whirled it round his head once, twice, three times, and let fly with one of the special stones he used for ammunition. He had hit the bear in the forehead, and the beast had crashed to the ground like a great tree blasted by

lightning. It was only afterwards that David had realised just how close to a grisly death he had come.

Time went past, and no news came. The days turned into weeks, and then one morning a messenger arrived.

David's brothers had almost run out of food and drink, and Eliab had sent the messenger to ask Jesse for more. David begged his father to let him take it to them, and Jesse eventually gave in, although he did make David promise to be careful.

CHAPTER TWO

STALEMATE

DAVID SET OFF, LEADING TWO packhorses loaded with food and drink. The next day he came to the Valley of Elah, where the two armies faced each other. David paused on a hill and gazed down.

The army of the Israelites was in a
camp on one slope of the valley, and on
the opposite slope was the army of the
Philistines. Some warriors on both sides
were warily watching each other, but most
just sat round their campfires or sheltered
in their tents from the heat of the sun.

It seemed very peculiar. This wasn't
what war was like in the stories David's
brothers liked to tell. He had expected to
see men fighting, and maybe even some
blood and gore. But absolutely nothing
was happening. David was intrigued, and
quickly descended with the packhorses.

The camp of the Israelites was very quiet, and David couldn't help noticing that most of the men seemed bored, and even rather miserable.

At last he came to the tents of his brothers. They were sitting round their campfire, not speaking. Then Eliab glanced up, saw David, and scowled at him.

"What are you doing here?" he growled.

18

"If you've run away without telling Father, you can go straight home. This is no place for little boys."

"I've brought the supplies you asked for," said David, nodding at the packhorses. "And what's the big deal? I don't see much going on that's dangerous. In fact, if I didn't know you men were supposed to be fighting against our deadliest enemies I'd think you were on holiday."

Eliab scowled at him more fiercely now, but he didn't disagree, and neither did any of the others. They glanced at each other, their cheeks burning with shame.

"It's very…complicated," Eliab said at last, and the others nodded in agreement. "Grown-up stuff, too difficult to explain to a kid like you."

"Try me," David murmured. He stood there waiting, arms folded.

So Eliab sighed, and told David what he wanted to know. It turned out that the two armies were evenly matched – neither side had enough men to be sure of defeating the other. So they had settled into an uneasy standoff. For forty days the Israelites had been unable to make the Philistines leave their land, and the Philistines had been unable to conquer it either.

"What are you going to do, then?" David said. "You can't just sit here waiting for the Philistines to leave. Doesn't the king have any ideas?"

"Who knows what goes through the great king's mind?" muttered Eliab, and the others all rolled their eyes. "Our strange and moody monarch hides in his tent with his priests and his fortune-tellers, hoping for a miracle. But one of the Philistines has been making a suggestion…"

Just then David heard a man start yelling in the distance. Each time the man paused there was a roar of many voices followed by a CRASH! "And there he is," Eliab said grimly.

"Right on time, as usual. Come and see, little brother."

Eliab and the others jumped to their feet and headed off in the direction of the noise. David went after them, and was soon part of a great throng of Israelites emerging from the camp and spreading out on their side of the valley. David pushed through to be at the front with his brothers.

And there before him on the opposite slope was a chilling sight. The Philistines had come out of their camp too, and were lined up for battle, their helmets and shields and the sharp points of their spears glittering in the sunlight. But one Philistine warrior stood in front of the rest.

CHAPTER THREE

GOLIATH

The Philistine was enormous beyond belief, much taller and broader than any man David had ever seen – a giant, in fact. He was wearing an immense brass helmet and gleaming armour, and carrying a huge sword and a shield the size of a cartwheel.

"Another day goes past," the giant called out. "And I, Goliath the Great, offer you Israelites the same challenge. Choose a champion to fight me in single combat!"

The Philistines roared, and beat their shields with their spears – CRASH!

"Let's put an end to this ridiculous standoff!" yelled Goliath, and there was another great roar and CRASH! "Winner takes all. Your champion wins – we leave. I win – WE RULE JUDEA FOREVER!"

The Philistines roared even more loudly, and yelled insults now too, calling the Israelites cowards and weaklings. David waited for a response from the warriors around him, but none came.

"What's wrong with everyone?" David said to Eliab. "Why doesn't somebody accept his challenge and shut that big idiot up for good?"

"Because it would be certain death, that's why," snapped Eliab. "Just look at him, David. There isn't a warrior here who could take him on and win. And who wants to be remembered as the man who lost our land?"

There was a murmur of agreement from David's brothers, and other men nearby.

David could hear Goliath still yelling, and the Philistine warriors banging their shields and laughing at the Israelites. Suddenly David's young heart grew hard against the warriors around him.

"You call yourselves men?" he said. "Well, I might only be a little boy, big brother, but I can see that Goliath is right in wanting to end all this hanging about. So I'll gladly accept his challenge. I'll be our champion."

"Don't…don't be ridiculous," spluttered Eliab. "You can't fight…"

"Who are you to say what he can't do?" a nearby warrior yelled. "Let him have a go if he wants. Anything is better than this endless waiting!"

Other voices were raised in agreement. Eliab argued with them, and with David, and someone finally said that they should let the king decide. So David was swept off by the mob and taken to the great tent of King Saul.

King Saul's dark eyes glittered when he heard what David had said. Silence descended once more on the Israelite warriors as they waited for their king to speak. A priest leaned over to whisper in one royal ear, then a fortune-teller in the other. And eventually…King Saul nodded.

"Perhaps I will have my miracle after all," he murmured. "Prepare the boy for battle."

Once more David was swept forward by the crowd, only this time to be strapped into the king's fine armour. The king's sword was thrust into his hand, and then he was hurried back to the valley slope, a huge crowd of warriors behind him.

Somebody shoved him out into the open ground, and he stood squinting in the sun, the king's helmet heavy on his head.

Goliath was just turning away, but one of the Israelites yelled at him.

"Wait, Goliath!" he said. "Our champion is here to fight you!"

CHAPTER FOUR
A BOY GOES OUT
TO BATTLE

GOLIATH PEERED ACROSS THE valley. David could see him grinning, and the Philistines pointing and nudging each other. Suddenly he felt his cheeks burning.

"Is that the best you can do?" yelled Goliath. "I like the fancy armour, but you should have chosen a man to fight me, not a little boy."

The Philistines roared with laughter now, and David couldn't blame them. Everything had happened so fast since he had volunteered to be the champion that he'd hardly had time to draw breath.

He realised now
that he must
look totally
ridiculous. The
king's armour was
simply too big for
him – the helmet kept slipping
down over his eyes, the breastplate hung
loose from his shoulders and he could
barely hold up the great shield.

An argument had broken out in the
Israelite ranks, somebody saying that it
was a stupid idea. And suddenly David
wondered what he was doing there, a boy
standing in a valley between two armies of
men, and he was tempted to run away and
hide behind his brothers.

But he knew that if he did, he would never be a man even if he grew to be taller than Goliath himself. Everyone would always think of him as the boy who had fled from the Philistine. He would have to fight him, here and now, as he had fought jackals and wolves and that bear. And thinking of how he'd dealt with the bear made David feel he could win... But he had to fight in the only way he knew how.

David threw the sword and shield down with a clatter, then pulled off the helmet and the breastplate and cast them aside too.

The Philistines laughed even more when they saw his slight, boyish figure, and Eliab called out. David ignored him  and walked forward, his head high.

He pulled out his sling, loaded it with a stone and kept it behind his back.

"Hey, Goliath!" he yelled, his voice just loud enough to be heard above the catcalls and laughter. "You wanted someone to fight. Well, fight me!"

"Go home, little boy," sneered Goliath, dismissing him with a wave of his huge hand and turning to go once more. "It's way past your bedtime!"

The Philistines jeered and laughed at him, but David kept advancing.

"What's wrong, you big ape?" he shouted. "Frightened I'll beat you?"

Goliath stopped, and swivelled on his heel. He glowered at David, and both armies fell silent. A sudden breeze blew dust round David's feet. He swallowed hard, tightened his grip on his sling and met the giant's gaze.

"I fear no one, man or boy," Goliath growled angrily. He raised his sword, hefted his shield and roared his war cry. "Prepare to die, Israelite!"

Then he came thundering down the valley slope, moving incredibly fast for a big man, the ground trembling as he ran. The Philistines cheered him on, and David heard Eliab yell, "Run for your life, David!"

But it was far too late for that. David ran towards Goliath instead, his eyes fixed on the giant's face, searching for the best spot to aim at. And there it was, a small area of skin between Goliath's eyebrows and his helmet rim.

They were almost in the bottom of the valley now, getting closer and closer. David could feel his heart pounding in his chest, his breath coming in gasps, but he also felt strangely calm. He whirled his sling once round his head, twice,

three times…then let fly, the stone
WHOOSHING through the air and
SMACKING into Goliath's forehead.

For an instant the giant simply looked
surprised. But soon his eyes rolled up
into his skull, and – like the bear – he
crashed to the ground and lay still.
A great gasp of disbelief and dismay
came from the Philistines. David slowly

walked over and nudged Goliath with his foot to make sure he was quite dead. He stood on the giant's back and held his sling aloft.

Then he roared his triumph to the sky, and his people roared too.

Eliab and his brothers came running out to him, and lifted him onto their shoulders. David smiled as he was acclaimed by the Israelites.

David's example helped the Israelite warriors find their courage – and the Philistines lose theirs. They were chased out of the valley, and right out of Judea. From then on David was a hero, and in due time he became a king far greater than Saul ever was, one with his own fine armour and weapons.

But that's another story.

And he will always be remembered for what he did that day, when he became David – the Boy Who Slew a Giant with a Little Stone!

DAVID AND GOLIATH
WINNING AGAINST
IMPOSSIBLE ODDS

BY TONY BRADMAN

The story of David and Goliath is very old. Some experts think it might be about events that took place nearly 3000 years ago. It first appeared in the collection of stories we know as *The Bible*. More precisely, it's in *The Old Testament*, most of which is about the early history of the Jewish people.

So the characters in the story – David and Goliath, King Saul, Jesse – may well have been real people. In fact *The Old Testament* is full of great stories and characters, and reading it helps us to know what it was like to live in those days. It also helps us to understand a lot about religion, too. Three of the world's great religious faiths – Judaism, Christianity and Islam – believe *The Bible* is holy.

But David's story has always been popular with people of every religion, and even those who don't believe in God at all. That's because we love stories about characters who win against impossible odds. Goliath is enormous, a grown-up and a warrior, and David is a mere boy – so nobody thinks he has a chance. He wins, though, and the surprise makes his victory even more impressive.

Like Robin Hood in his struggle with the evil Sheriff of Nottingham, or the boy Aladdin in his encounter with a powerful magician, David is an underdog. The villain has all the power and the strength, as villains often do – but the hero has a skill which he can use to win. Aladdin has his wits, as does Robin Hood. But Robin and David also have other skills – courage and a deadly aim.

David keeps his cool and proves that the small and weak can beat the strong and powerful – whether it's a young hero in the ancient Middle East, or a team from a lower league beating the champions. It's a story that speaks to us all.

It makes us feel that we could take on the bad people, the bullies of this world – and win. This story will be loved so long as there are bullies to defeat!

THE GREATEST ADVENTURES IN THE WORLD

TONY BRADMAN & TONY ROSS